Writer
Pat Mills

Artist
Olivier Ledroit

Lettering
Charlotte Reilly

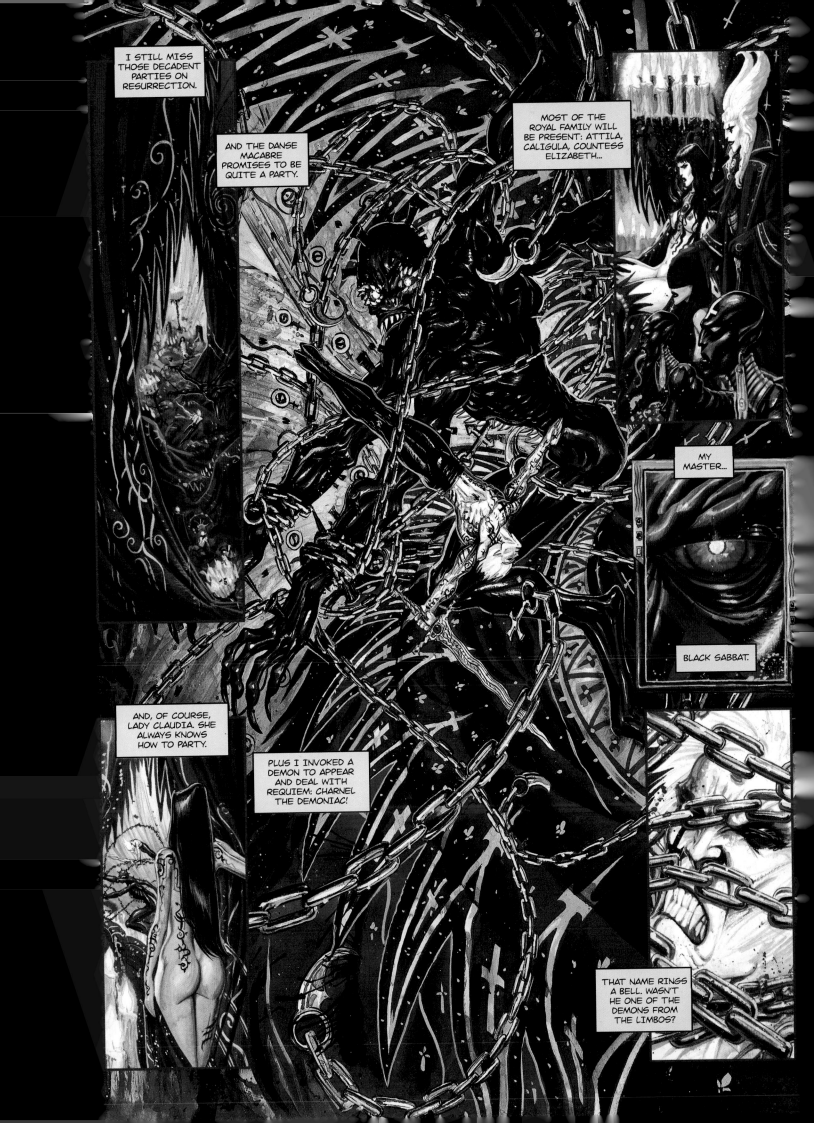

IT'S ARMED WITH WEAPONS FROM EVERY EARTH ERA, INCLUDING DEMONICALLY GUIDED IMPALERS, KLESA CLUSTER BOMBS, TRACTOR BEAMS...

AND THREE DOOMSDAY MEN.

YOU ARE REPELLED BY THE CRUCIFIXIONS...? I WOULD NOT WANT ANYONE IN MY SERVICE WHO WAS REPELLED BY TORTURE.
NO! I'M REALLY ENJOYING WATCHING MY PRIESTS BURN!
THEN WHY ARE YOU UPSET?
I... I'M UPSET WITH THE HIEROPHANTS FOR DARING TO QUESTION YOUR JUDGEMENT, SIRE!
ARE YOU CERTAIN? WE COULD DISCUSS THIS IN THE ORIFICIUM IF YOU PREFER?
NO, NO! THERE'S REALLY NO NEED.
THAT'S WHERE ALL THE ASSHOLES ARE, YOU KNOW.
OR RIGHT HERE! THERE'S A TORTURE CHAIR READY AND WAITING FOR YOU.
ALL YOU HAVE TO DO IS...
OPEN WIDE...
ONLY WE'RE NOT SURE WHICH END YET...

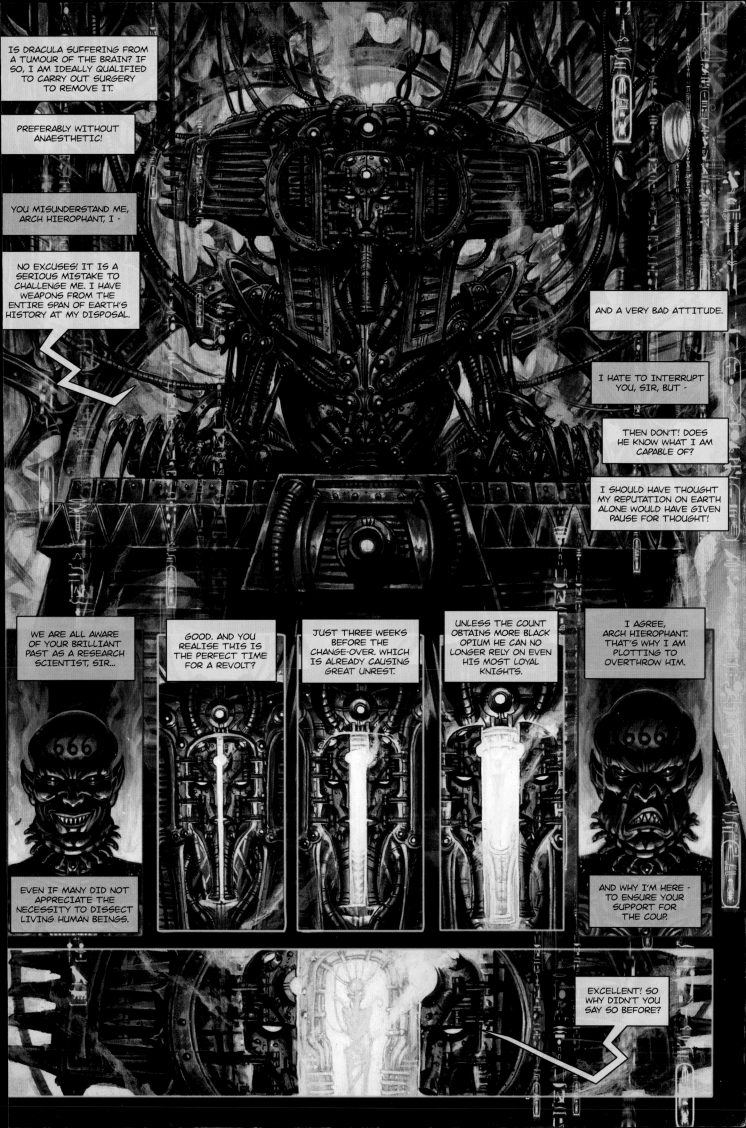

NOW. CONSIDER HOW DRACONIA IS SURROUNDED BY HOSTILE LANDS... IN THE WEST: ZOMBIA, TERRA VOODOO AND THE OTHER DISUNITED STATES OF THE ATLANTIC.

IN THE NORTH: PANDEMONIUM, LEMURIA AND DYSTOPIA. IN THE SOUTH: HADES AND TARTARUS.

WHILE TO THE EAST IS OUR REALM OF THANATOS AND THE MAGEDOMS OF KABALIA AND CYCLOPIA

DRACULA HAS MADE ENEMIES IN EVERY ONE OF THESE LANDS. THEY WILL ALL SUPPORT REGIME CHANGE...

THERE ARE ALSO THE SKY PIRATES TO CONSIDER. MITRA HAS PROMISED AN AERIAL ASSAULT ON THE CAPITAL.

AND I HAVE LEARNT DRACULA IS TRYING TO GET EMERGENCY SUPPLIES OF BLACK OPIUM FROM ATLANTIS. MITRA HAS PROMISED TO INTERCEPT THE SUPPLY TRAIN.

I SHALL CAUSE A RUN ON THE LITRE. THE PROSPECT OF A BLOOD SHORTAGE, AS WELL AS OPIUM, SHOULD LEAD TO RIOTS IN THE STREETS.

ONCE DRACULA IS OVERTHROWN, HE WILL BE REPLACED BY LORD CRYPTOS HEADING A GOVERNMENT OF NATIONAL UNITY.

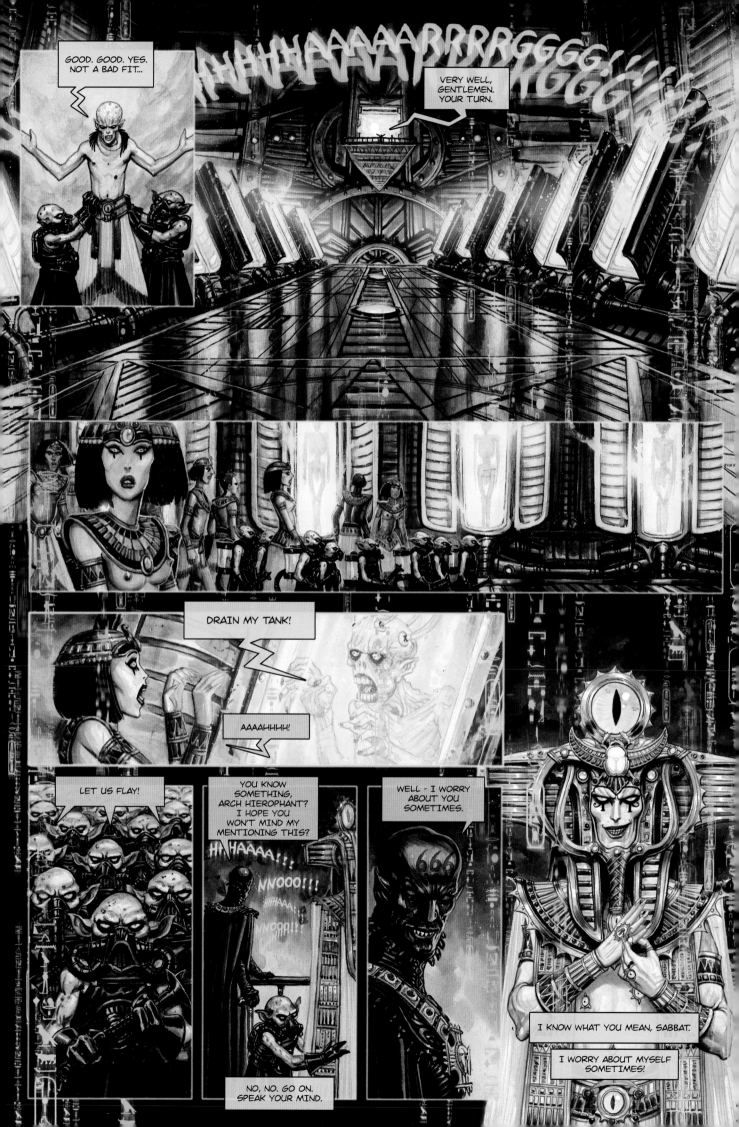

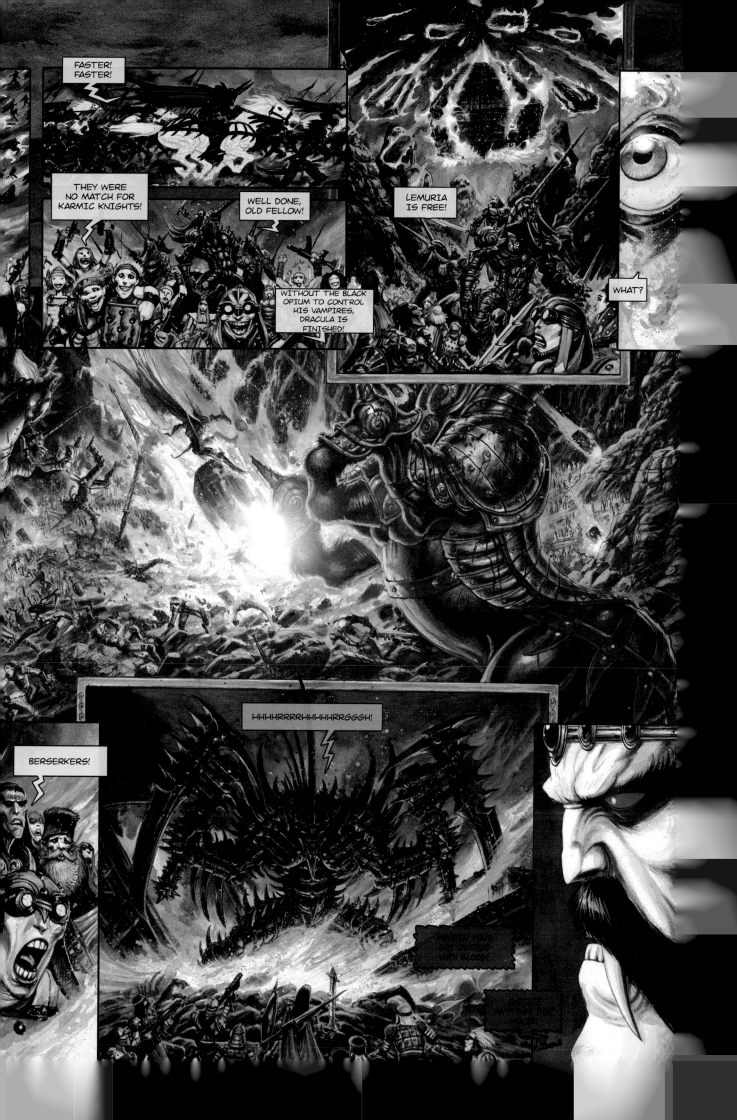

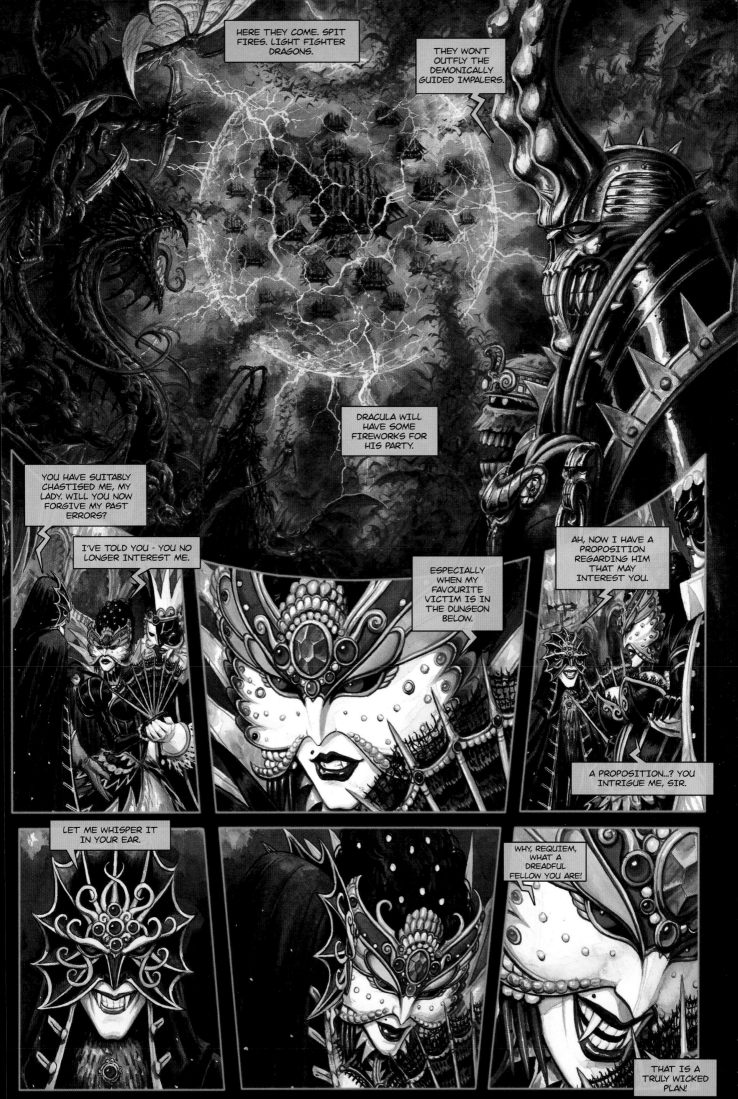

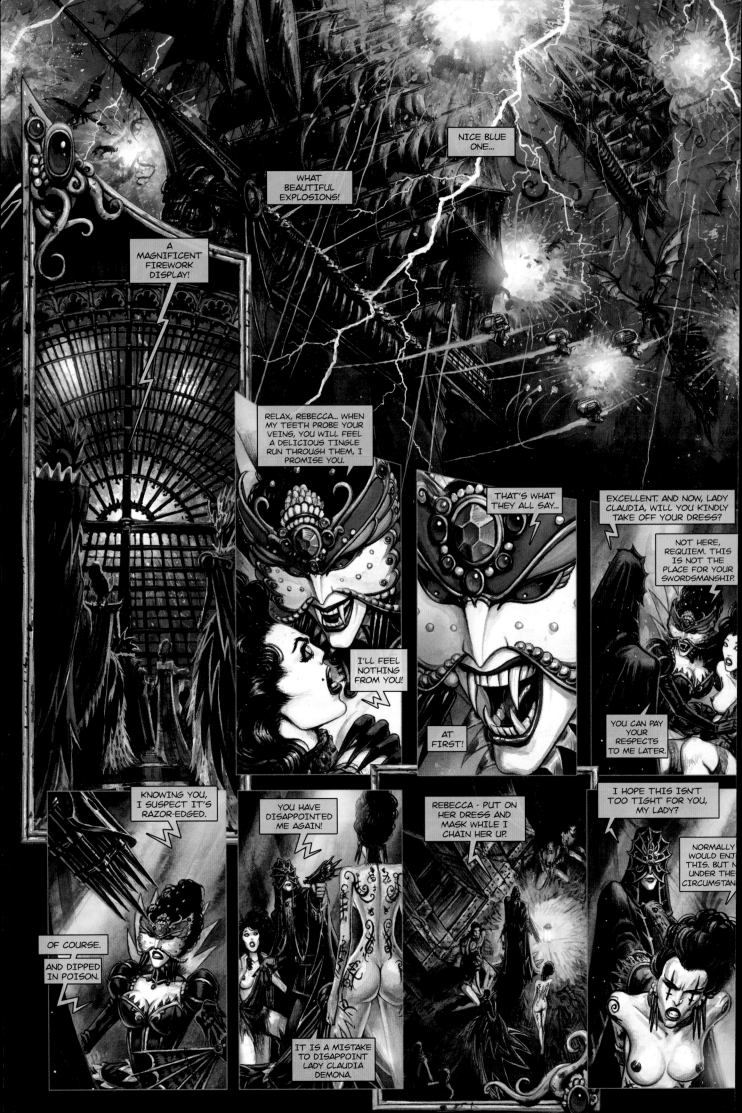

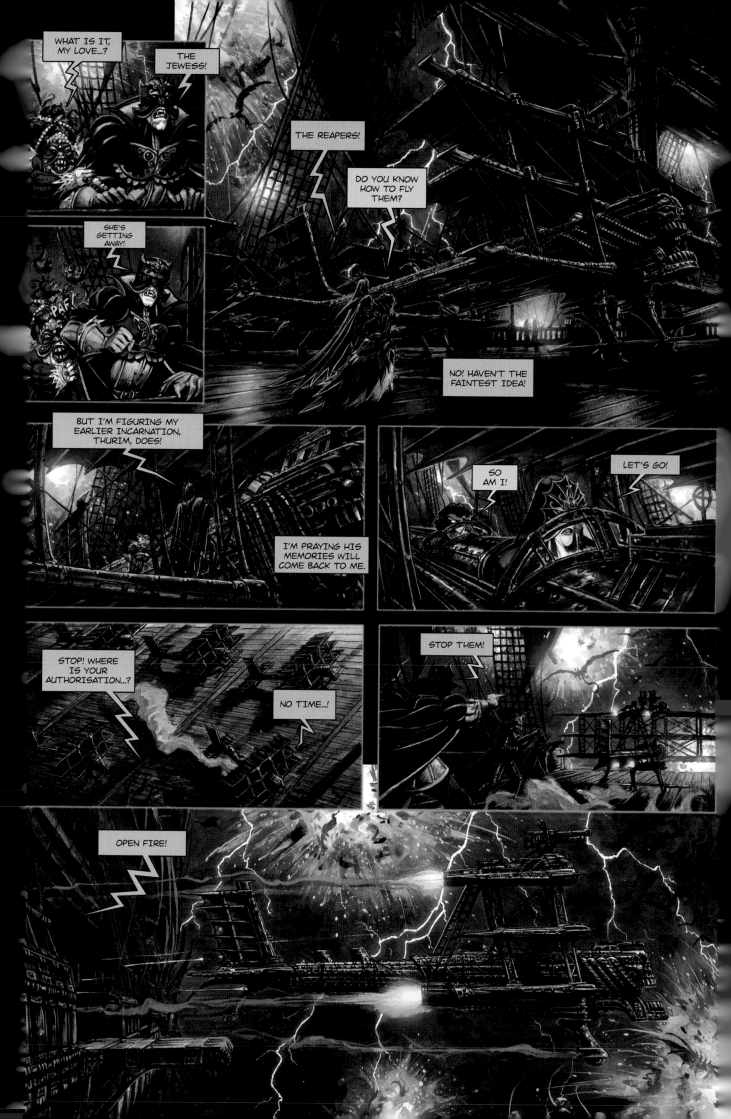

GALLERY OF THE DAMNED

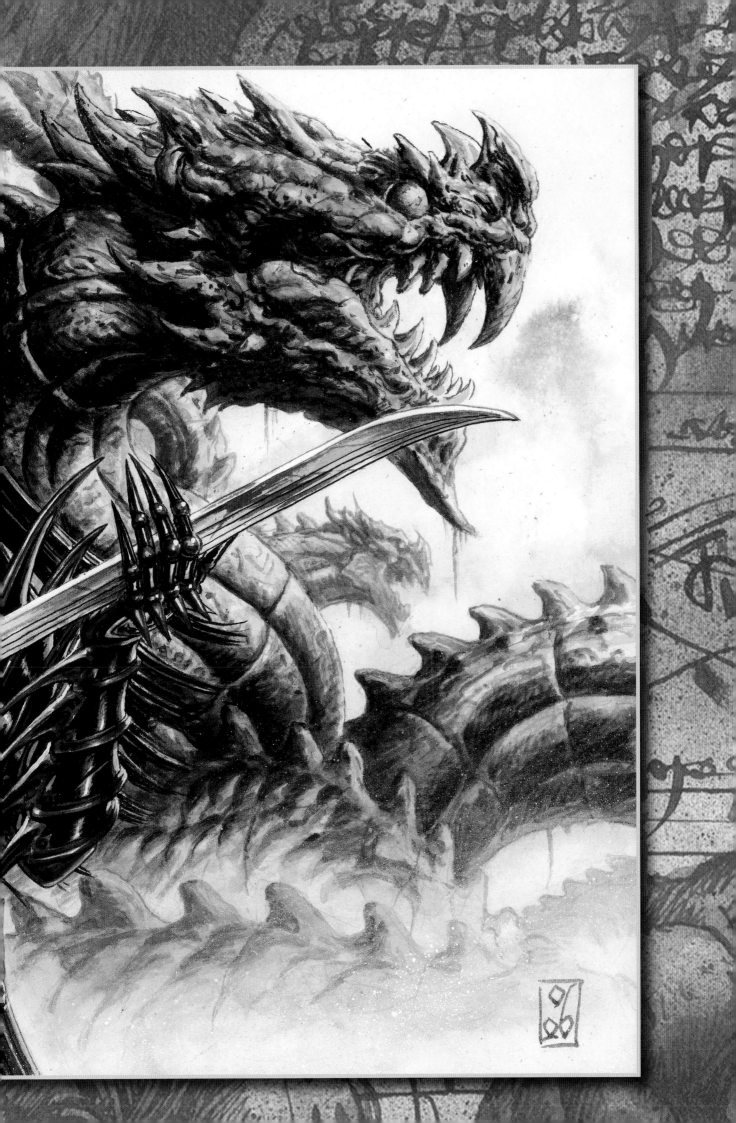